Library of Congress Control Number: 2019936874

CIP data is available.

ISBN-10: 0-8198-3156-5   ISBN-13: 978-0-8198-3156-9

Originally published in English as *Guess Who's in the Manger!*

First North American edition, 2019

Published by Pauline Books & Media, 50 Saint Paul's Avenue, Boston, MA 02130-3491

Printed in Malaysia

GWITM TLPLHK555555100010 3156-5

www.pauline.org

Pauline Books & Media is the publishing house of the Daughters of St. Paul, an international congregation of women religious serving the Church with the communications media.

1 2 3 4 5 6 7 8 9   23 22 21 20 19

Guess Who's in the Manger?

A Christmas Story

Written by Vicki Howie
Illustrated by Julia Seal

Perched high on a rafter,
a barn owl gazed down,
at his dreary shelter,
in Bethlehem town.

That stable was dark.
It was bare; it was poor!
No wonder few visitors stepped
through the door . . .

. . . just the kind innkeeper
bringing fresh straw!
HEE HAW . . .
HEE HAW . . .

The barn owl was lonely,
and blinked in the gloom,

If only a light would burn bright in that room,
a friend might drop in to say,
"How do you do?"
But only the ox at the
manger breathed, "Moo!"
MOO . . . MOO . . .

Then one afternoon, what a din from the street,
a clatter of hooves and a patter of feet,
a crowd at the inn made a hullabaloo!
"A bed for the night!"
"Have you room for us, too?"

"We've traveled so far, any shelter will do.
We're Joseph and Mary—our baby is due!"

The ox and the donkey were wise to it all.
To owl they explained as they lay in their stall.
They told of a promise God made long ago,
that a light would come to those
dark streets—and GLOW!

"I'll hunt for that light!"
screeched the barn owl. "Goodbye!"
He stretched out his wings
and rose into the sky.
TWIT TWOO . . . TWIT TWOO . . .

The owl met the cherry-red
sun, sinking low,
"Great light, won't you shine
in my stable below?"

"Not me!" said the big sun,
"I'm King of the Day.
I'm off to wake people
in lands far away!"

The owl begged the
wispy-white moon, riding high,
"Great light, come
and shine in my stable nearby!"
"Not I!" said the cool moon,
"I'm Queen of the Night,
I gaze at the town
from a very great height!"

The owl cried in anguish, but as he swooped low,
over shepherds in fields with campfires aglow,
he heard, amid the clouds, many angels sing,
"Guess who's in the manger! Turn, turn on the wing!"

“Oh, don’t be afraid,
little owl, do not frown,
All Glory to God,
for bright love has come down!”

Bewildered, the barn owl flew back to the town.
The streets were deserted; the shutters were down.
He dived to his stable and stared when he saw,
the rays of gold light that streamed out the old door!

Led on by that glorious light, the owl flew,
to perch on the manger and gaze at the view.

There lay a sweet baby
whose bright smiling face,
lit up every nook in that
once dreary place!
WHO . . . WHO . . ?

And soon many visitors flocked through the door,
to see the new baby and kneel in the straw,

And even the creatures said,
"How do you do?"
To God's only Son—baby Jesus, that's who!!
COO . . . COO . . .

Perched high on a rafter,
the barn owl looked around,
at his cheerful shelter,
in Bethlehem town.

He puffed out
his feathers and
danced in the light
that God sent to earth
on that first Christmas night!
WHOO . . . HOO . . .
WHOO . . . HOO!